BLACK BELT
PRO FITNESS

This is a work of fiction. Names, characters, places, and and incidents either are a product of the author's imagination or are used fictisiously. Any resemblence to actual persons, living or dead, events, or locales is entirely coincidental.

Copyright © 2020/2021 by Chris Hershberger

All right reserved. No part of this book may be reproduced or used in any manner without written permission of the copyright owner except for the use of quotation in a book review.

Book illustrated and designed by Eric Spayde
ISBN 978-0-578-85991-0

Published by Black Belt Pro Fitness, LLC
Address
1099 West Fourth St. Mansfield, Ohio 44906

Website
www.jrblackbelts.com

This book is dedicated to my Martial Arts Family.

You have inspired me every step of my journey.
-Chris Hershberger

One virtual lesson on us!

"Uh oh! Looks like Justin's in trouble again!"

FRONT KICK!!

FRONT KICK !!

FRONT KICK !!

FRONT KICK!!

SIDE KICK !!

ROUNDHOUSE!!

ROUNDHOUSE !!

ONE WEEK LATER...

Grace D.
- 5x National Champion
- 2x International Champion

Favorite Techniques
- Flying Side Kick
- High Side Kick

Team Great Britain

Natalie H.
- 8x National Champion
- 6x International Champion

Favorite Techniques
-High Roundhouse
-Axe Kick

Team USA

"I'm glad to know my training prepared me for the international championship title!"

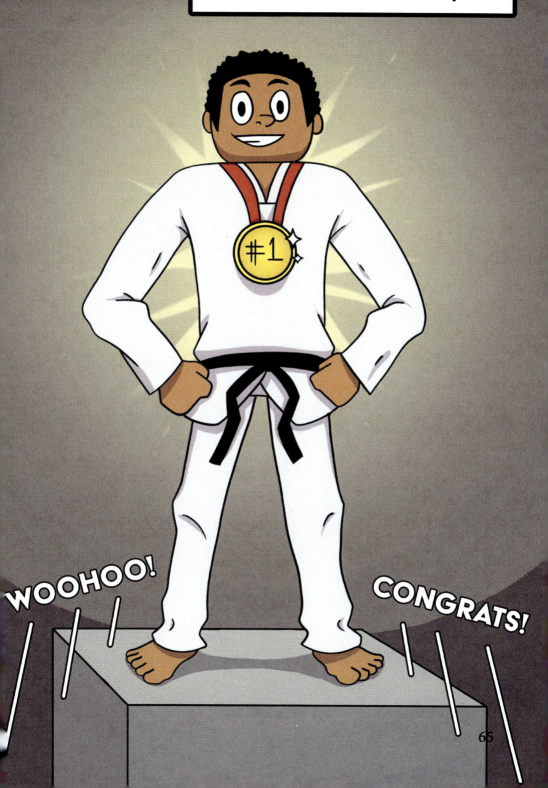

One virtual lesson on us!

Made in the USA
Columbia, SC
09 December 2021